LEVEL 2 READER

Pokémon™

Ash Takes the Cake

Adapted by Maria S. Barbo

SCHOLASTIC INC.

ISBN 978-1-339-02803-3

10 9 8 7 6 5 4 3 2 1   24 25 26 27 28

Printed in the U.S.A. 40

First printing 2024

Designed by Cheung Tai

"This cake is tasty!" Ash said with his mouth full.

Ash, Goh, and Chloe were on their way to battle the Gym Leader Opal.

But first they needed a snack!

The friends were at a bakery where the chef's Alcremie made all the cream.

"The happier the Alcremie, the sweeter the cream!" Chloe said.

Something white nuzzled Goh's cheek.

"Is that a Pokémon?" Chloe asked. "It's so cute!"

"It's a Milcery," Ash said. "Its body is made of cream!"

Goh caught the Cream Pokémon with his Poké Ball.

"Mil! Mil!" Milcery cheered.

"We'll be good friends!" Goh said.

Chloe's Eevee sniffed Milcery.
It smelled good!
Goh's Grookey licked
Milcery's cheek.
It tasted good!
Grookey and Eevee
chased Milcery
around the table.

"Stop!" Chloe shouted.

"I'm sorry, Milcery," Goh said.

He gave Milcery the strawberry from his cake.

Then he twirled his new Pokémon in the air!

Milcery began to glow.
"Could it be?" Ash said, amazed.
Was Milcery evolving into Alcremie?

Ash read from his Pokédex.

"Milcery evolves by twirling around and around. Just like mixing cream."

"It must have been happy to get that strawberry!" Chloe said.

Goh smiled at his new Alcremie.
"We'll really be good friends!" he said.
"Hey!" Ash shouted. "We're late for the Gym!"

"Opal, we made it!" Ash called as they ran into the Gym.

Opal opened her arms wide.

"Welcome to the very first Alcremie decoration challenge!" she said.

"Huh?" Ash asked. "No battling?"

"Each Trainer will team up with an Alcremie to decorate a cake," Opal said. "Fasten your seat belts!"

Goh chose to work with his own Alcremie.

Ash and Chloe chose from Opal's team of Alcremie.

"I never knew there were so many colors and flavors!" Ash said.

Chloe picked a yellow Alcremie with pink hearts.
Ash used his nose to choose a Caramel Swirl Alcremie.

"This smell is the one I like the best," he said.

"Let's go!" Opal said.
The contest had begun!
Each Alcremie filled a bowl with whipped cream.
Each Trainer spread the cream on their cake.

Then it was time to decorate!
"Pikachu, you're up!" Ash said.
Pikachu used its tail to swat toppings at Ash.
Ash plunked them on their cake.

Chloe's cake looked delicious!

Goh's cake also looked delicious—to Grookey.

The Chimp Pokémon licked off all the cream!

"Will you stop snacking?!" Goh begged.

"Everybody, look at my cake!" Ash called. "Tada!"

Goh cringed. Chloe smiled.

Ash's cake had LOTS of toppings.

"That's so totally Ash!" Chloe said.

"This looks creative," Opal said about
Ash's cake.

She took a bite and her eyes opened wide.
"Fun-tastic!" she shouted.

Opal pointed at Ash. "You're the one
I will battle!"

"Battle?!" Ash asked.

"A Trainer who made such an interesting
cake MUST be fun to battle!" Opal said.

"What are you waiting for?" Opal said. "Take your places!"

Ash's Pikachu faced Opal's Alcremie.

Chloe and Goh cheered from the stands.
"You've got this!" they shouted.

"Pikachu, use Iron Tail!" Ash said.
Pikachu slammed Alcremie with one Iron Tail
after another.

"Excellent job, Pikachu!" Ash shouted.

"Please look at your Pokémon closely," Opal said.

"Huh?" Ash asked.

Ash looked at Pikachu's tail.
It was covered in pink cream!
"The cream that piled up on its tail takes away
Iron Tail's power!" Goh said.

"Our turn," Opal said. "Alcremie, use Attract."
Pink hearts shot out of Alcremie's eyes.
They made Pikachu dizzy.
Then Alcremie blasted Pikachu with Dazzling Gleam.

No!" cried Ash. "Can you go on, buddy?"
Pikachu slowly stood up, then sent a move back.

"I'm going to have fun with this," Opal said.
She threw out a giant Poké Ball.
Gigantamax Alcremie filled the arena.

"G Max Finale!" Opal shouted.
The sky turned purple.
Lightning struck.
Giants blobs of cream crashed
down around Pikachu.

Pikachu dodged some of the cream comets, and ate others!

The Mouse Pokémon grew bigger and bigger.

"Pikachu Gigantamaxed!" Goh shouted.

"Pikachu, use G-Max Volt Crash!" Ash called.

"Pika!" Pikachu pounded its belly . . . and **burped**.

Pikachu had not Gigantamaxed.
It ate so much cream, it had FEAST-amaxed!
"My goodness," said Opal. "Battle's over!"

The group celebrated their big day by trying all the cakes they had made.

"Whoa, this is delish!" Goh said.

But that was no surprise. Everything tastes sweeter with friends!